Danny's Monster

By Laura Lyth

Illustrated by David Hearn

This is Danny.

Danny has a pet monster, he is so small that he climbs into Danny's pocket and sits with Danny all day.

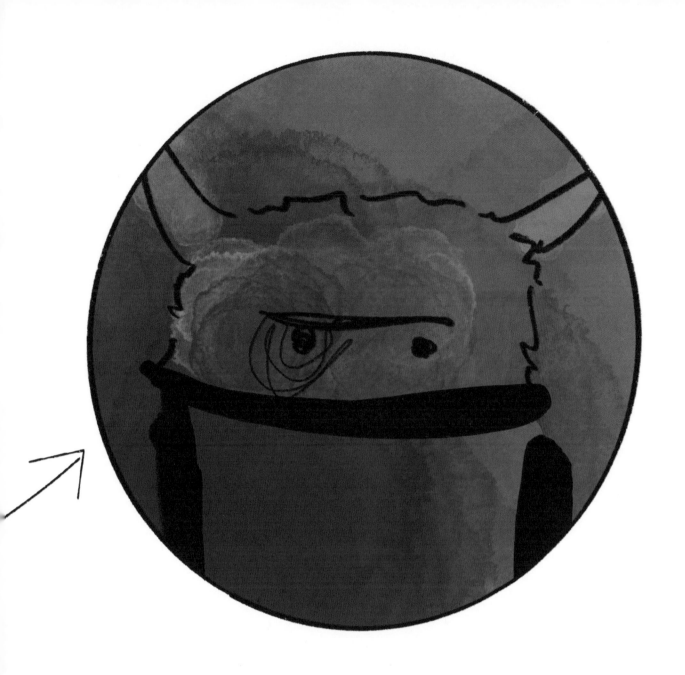

Monster is very small, he doesn't say much but he feels sad. This makes Danny feel sad too, but it's okay because Monster is so small he is easy to ignore.

Every day, Monster grows a
little bit bigger

and gets a
little bit louder.

One day Danny notices that
Monster doesn't fit quietly
inside his pocket anymore.

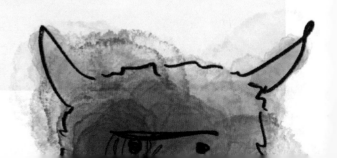

Monster takes up all the space; he is so big that Danny can't see past it.

As Monster grows,

he gets louder

and louder.

He shouts at Danny and tells

him things that makes

Danny feel scared and sad.

Danny decides to play loud music to drown out the sound of the Monster.

He bangs on his drums.

BASH! BANG!

He blows into his recorder so hard that his cheeks turn purple.

WHISTLE! WHISTLE!

Danny turns up the music as loud as he can, but the louder Danny plays, the louder Monster shouts. "It's no good", thinks Danny, "I can't get Monster to be quiet". Then he has another idea...

Danny runs from the Monster.

But, however fast Danny runs,

Monster always catches him.

Danny feels overwhelmed looking after such a big Monster all by himself, so he asks a grown up for help.

"Your Monster makes you feel sad", Danny's grown up says. "Yes", replies Danny. Danny cries. Danny is sad and Danny is brave.

Danny thinks it isn't fair how this Monster has
shown up and is making him feel so horrible.
Danny feels angry. He **screams.**
Danny is **angry** and Danny is brave.

"It's okay to feel sad and angry", says Danny's grown up, "and it's okay to cry". Danny's grown up tells him that he doesn't have to face the Monster alone anymore, this feels nice. Danny smiles.

Now that Danny knows he isn't alone, he stops
trying to hide from the monster, he stops running
and he stops trying to get the Monster to be quiet.

Danny asks Monster where he has come from
and what he needs.

But Monster is too big and scary, Danny doesn't
understand him. Danny realises that sometimes
monsters don't live under your bed, sometimes
monsters live inside your head.

Danny tries hard to listen to the Monster and to get to know him. He realises that the more time he spends with the Monster, the less scary he becomes.

So Danny gives Monster attention.

Danny sits with his Monster.

Danny listens to what Monster wants and is kind to Monster. Sometimes Monster wants to take naps and cuddle up under the blankets, sometimes Monster wants to get outside and go for walks.

Danny and Monster make friends. Danny isn't afraid anymore.

Danny and the Monster go to bed. Monster smiles. Danny has never seen monster smile before.

"Thank you for spending time with me and for listening to what I had to say Danny", says Monster, "you were very brave". Danny smiles too, and he falls asleep cuddling Monster.

The next morning Danny wakes up with the sun shining on his face. Monster has gone.

Today is a new day.

Danny doesn't feel sad anymore. He knows that monsters visit but they don't stay. Danny knows that it is okay to have sad days and angry days. Danny knows that it is okay to have happy days and silly days, filled with fun.

Danny opens the curtains and looks out of the window, "Thank you for teaching me, Monster!" Shouts Danny.

Many miles away, Monster sits alone in a beautiful meadow. He hears Danny's call, and he smiles.

This book was created to help promote
better mental health in children and enable
them to grow with the message "it's okay
to feel and it's brave to do so."

Dedicated to my brother, Alex Lyth, who
told me I should write shortly before losing
his own battle and life to mental health.

U.K. helpline numbers

CALM - 0800 58 58 58
PAPYRUS - 0800 068 41 41
Samaritans - 116 123
Saneline - 0300 304 7000
YoungMinds 0808 802 5544
Anxiety UK - 03444 775 774
Mind - 0300 123 3393
No Panic - 0300 772 9844
OCD Action - 0845 390 6232
Rethink Mental Illness - 0300 5000 927

U.S. helpline numbers

Crisis text line - text "hello" to 741741
Central Valley Suicide Prevention Hotline - 1 (888) 506-5991
TeenLine - (310) 855-4673 or text "teen" to 839863

Special thanks to Bradley and Edison for your encouragement, support and love.

Thank you to my illustrator, Dave Hearn, for your patience, creativity and talent.

Thank you to my brother, Alex Lyth,for inspiring me every day to follow my dreams.

Printed in Poland
by Amazon Fulfillment
Poland Sp. z o.o., Wrocław

86691819R00018